Flowers for You

Blooms for Every Month

by

Anita Holmes

Illustrated by

Virginia Wright-Frierson

Bradbury Press   New York

Maxwell Macmillan Canada   Toronto
Maxwell Macmillan International
New York   Oxford   Singapore   Sydney

To Deirdre Elizabeth Holmes
—A. H.

To Helen Duckson Wright
and Marshall Sheldon Wright,
and
To Josephine Daniels Frierson
and George Dargan Frierson,
with thanks to Sharon Steinhoff
—V. W.-F.

The illustrations were done on hot-pressed Fabriano watercolor paper using pencil and watercolor. The artist works directly from life at all times and has for many years taken an especial interest in rendering flowers. The illustrations were color-separated by scanner and reproduced in four colors using red, blue, yellow, and black inks.

Library of Congress Cataloging-in-Publication Data   Holmes, Anita.   Flowers for you: Blooms for every month / by Anita Holmes; pictures by Virginia Wright-Frierson. — 1st American ed.   p.   cm.   Summary: Describes a variety of flowering plants and what it takes to grow them successfully indoors.   ISBN 0–02–744280–2   1. House plants — Juvenile literature. 2. Flowers — Juvenile literature. 3. Indoor gardening — Juvenile literature. [1. Indoor gardening. 2. Gardening.] I. Wright-Frierson, Virginia, ill. II. Title. SB419.2.H65   1993 635.9′65 — dc20   91-9482

Contents

Introduction

Do you love flowers? Most people do. Throughout history, people have been fascinated by flowers. A bouquet is lovely. But it only lasts for a short while. A flowering plant, on the other hand, can brighten our surroundings for weeks and weeks — or even months and months.

Before you can successfully grow flowers indoors, you need to know something about flowers and their needs. Also, what flowers should you buy? Where should you put them? How do you take care of them? And what choice of plants will give you blooms year-round? You'll find the answers inside this book.

In the beginning you will find general tips on choosing flowering plants and growing them indoors. A section in the middle introduces you to twelve special plants, with instructions on how to care for them. For ambitious gardeners, there are guidelines at the back of the book for potting and multiplying plants, as well as troubleshooting tips and other information.

What Is a Flower?

Look through the pages of this book. You can see that flowers come in many shapes, sizes, and colors. Some grow one to a stem. Some grow in clusters. Some have huge, showy petals. Others have small, delicate petals. Flowers add beauty to our world. But they also have a special purpose — to produce seeds. Flowers are the seed-producing part of the plant. And from seeds come new plants.

Here is a drawing of a typical flowering plant. What are the main parts of the plant? Do you know how each part helps the plant live and produce other plants?

To thrive, you need food and water, air, and protection from extreme heat and cold. Tender loving care — and a bath now and then — also help.

Plants also have these basic needs. All flowering plants need soil and water and a healthy environment. For a plant this means plenty of fresh air, warmth, and sunlight.

All plants have these same needs. But they need them in different amounts. Some plants, for instance, need lots of water while others need just a little. Some need full sunlight all day long while others need just a few hours of sun.

What about food? In a process called photosynthesis, green plants turn energy from the sun (sunlight is a form of energy), gases from the air, and chemical elements from water into food. Foodmaking takes place in the leaves of most plants. Sunlight is absorbed by the leaves; air enters plants through tiny holes in their leaves; and water is collected by the plants' roots and carried through their stems to the leaves.

Out-of-doors, nature gives plants enough sunlight, air, and water to thrive. Indoors, you, the gardener, must provide the healthy environment. So before you choose a plant to grow, find out what its growing needs are. Also, do a little detective work to make sure you can give the plant the proper environment.

Check Out the Environment

You wouldn't plant a moisture-loving forest plant in a dry desert. Likewise, you shouldn't try to grow a moisture-loving houseplant in a desert-like room. Here are some questions to ask when trying to match a plant to an indoor space.

How's the Light?

To produce buds, most flowering plants need at least four hours of sun a day. Some need more. A few can thrive in a shady spot as long as it is bright. No flowering plant can do well in a place that is too dim to read in.

How can you judge the brightness of a spot in a room? First, notice where the windows are and what direction they face.

The sunniest spot in a room is in or near a south-facing window. It gives four hours or more of direct sunlight a day. The dimmest is the north-facing window. It is always shady. An east-facing window gives about four hours of morning sun — thus, it is partly sunny. A west-facing window lets in about four hours of afternoon sun — it, too, is partly sunny. Any window becomes shady when covered by curtains or blinds.

You can add brightness to a room with artificial light. Many gardeners use special plant-growing lamps or bulbs for part or all of the day. Almost as good and not so expensive are fluorescent lamps and bulbs. You may have a desk lamp with a fluorescent bulb you can use.

Keep an artificial light at least eight inches from your plant — close enough to do some good, but not so close as to burn it. If the leaves of the plant curl under, the light is too close.

How's the Temperature?

Most people are comfortable in a room that is between 68°F and 75°F during the day and 55°F and 65°F at night. This "medium" temperature range is just right for many flowering plants as well. Some, however, prefer slightly warmer or slightly cooler temperatures.

What's the temperature range in your room? One way to find out is to use a thermometer. Take a reading in the middle of the day and then again in the morning, before the heat is turned up. If you don't have a thermometer, you can do your own "comfort check."

Don't worry about a few degrees above or below "medium," for instance, or panic if the room occasionally gets colder or hotter than normal. But do watch out for temperature extremes. Plants should be kept away from radiators and heaters, unless they are set on a pebble tray. And no plants should be kept in front of frosty windows, drafty doors, or air conditioners. In winter, you can protect your plants from window drafts by pulling a window shade or curtain behind them at night.

TEMPERATURE CHART

	Temperature Range	Comfort Check
WARM	Over 75°F days Over 65°F nights	Don't need sleeves — days Sheet or light blanket — nights
MEDIUM	68°-75°F days 55°-65°F nights	Sleeves feel comfortable — days Need a warm blanket — nights
COOL	Less than 68°F days Less than 55°F nights	Need a sweater — days Several blankets — nights

How's the Humidity?

Have you noticed that in winter your skin and lips can get dry and chapped? This dryness is caused by low humidity. Humidity is the moisture found in air.

Most flowering plants do not do well in low humidity. Low humidity causes leaves to grow poorly or turn yellow. It can also cause plants to wilt or drop their leaves. Here are some tips to help you decide whether your rooms are dry or humid.

A room is probably dry if
…the climate outside is dry and windows are open.
…the room is heated by a heater, radiator, or fireplace.
…the room is cooled by an air conditioner.

A room is probably fairly humid if
…the climate outside is humid and windows are open.
…a humidifier is in the room.
…the room is filled with leafy plants.

Can you make up for low humidity in a room? Yes, indeed. Since plants give off water vapor through their leaves, you can group them together in one spot so they'll make the area around them more humid. Setting a plant on a pebble tray is another solution. Fill a tray or large saucer with pebbles or coarse gravel. Set your plant, or plants, on the pebbles. Then cover the pebbles with water. Make sure the water does not come up over the bottom of the pots, or the plants will drown. Add water each day as it evaporates.

Choosing Your Plant

Today's the day you're going shopping for a flowering plant. Now that you know what kind of light, temperature, and humidity you can give a plant, you are ready to choose a plant to grow. Use the chart on the next page to help you select some plants that will do well in your environment.

Suppose, for instance, that you have a warm, fairly dry room with an east-facing window. Looking at the chart, you can see that an orchid cactus would be a good choice for your partly sunny, warm, and fairly dry spot. If you can increase the humidity in the room, you can also grow a hibiscus, a spathiphyllum, or a wax begonia.

The twelve popular flowering plants featured in this book are fairly easy to grow, but some are easier than others. The easiest to grow are the hibiscus, wax begonia, orchid cactus, strawberry geranium, shrimp plant, and spathiphyllum. The others are not difficult, but you need to know some tricks about getting them to bloom.

A few of the plants included in this book bloom year-round. Most, however, flower in one season only. By choosing one or two plants for each season, you can have flowers twelve months of the year.

Where can you purchase flowering plants? Try a good flower shop, garden center, nursery, or even a large supermarket. Before you pay for your selection, check it over carefully. Make sure the plant is healthy and well shaped. Examine its leaves and stems to make sure there are no tiny insect pests hiding there.

Be Prepared

If you don't already have some basic gardening supplies on hand, you might also buy a watering can, fertilizer, a drainage saucer, and a small trowel when you purchase your plant. Other items you may need later on include extra soil, pots, plastic bags, crockery, pebbles, and wooden stakes. Keep all your gardening supplies together in a box. In your box you might also keep index cards on how to care for each of your plants.

summer

fall

Plant Chart

winter

spring

NAME	BLOOMING SEASON	ENVIRONMENT NEEDS			CARE COMMENTS
		LIGHT	TEMPERATURE	HUMIDITY	
African violet	Year-round	Partly sunny	Warm	High	Give additional light in winter for blooms.
Amaryllis	Spring	Partly sunny	Warm, day; Cool, night	Medium	Dormant in fall. Store bulb in cool spot.
Christmas cactus	Winter	Bright sunless or partly sunny	Cool	Medium	Short-day plant. Keep on the moist side.
Chrysanthemum	Fall	Sunny	Warm, day; Cool, night	High	Propagate in spring for fall blooms.
Geranium	Nearly year-round	Sunny	Medium, day	Medium	Propagate often for year-round blooms.
Hibiscus	Year-round	Partly sunny	Warm	High	Keep moist or buds may drop.
Kalanchoe	Winter	Sunny	Cool to medium	Medium	Short-day plant.
Orchid cactus	Spring	Partly sunny	Medium, day; Cool, night	Medium	Keep on the moist side.
Shrimp plant	Summer	Sunny	Warm	Medium	Remove colorful bracts as they fade.
Spathiphyllum	Fall	Bright sunless or partly sunny	Medium to warm	High	Keep moist.
Strawberry geranium	Summer	Partly sunny	Cool	Medium to high	Put in hanging pot.
Wax begonia	Year-round	Partly sunny	Medium	Medium to high	In northern areas, may rest in winter.

Loving Care

Choosing a plant is one thing; taking care of it is another. However, loving care is not difficult to give if you just follow a few basic guidelines. The instructions on the next pages will help you, but don't worry if you can't follow them exactly. Gardening is not an exact science. A sunny window in one house is different from a sunny window in another. Also, soils differ, pots differ, fertilizers differ, and certainly, plants differ. So a good gardener must be a good observer and follow his or her hunches. If your plants are healthy, keep up the good work. If they are not doing well, try to figure out why. Don't give up if you make a mistake or two. Gardeners become good by trial and error!

Watering and Misting

top watering

bottom watering

misting

A plant is ninety percent water. If a plant doesn't take in water as it uses it, the plant will wilt and eventually die. On the other hand, too much water can kill a plant. Soil cannot hold air when it is soggy. Without air, plant roots drown and rot. Plants use lots of water on sunny days, especially during their growing seasons, or periods of rapid growth. They need very little during their resting periods.

You can tell that your plant needs water when its soil feels barely damp or dry. Water your plant by filling the pot to the top of its rim. Use lukewarm, not cold, water. As soon as water runs into the drainage saucer, you have given your plant enough to drink. After watering, empty the drainage saucer so the plant is not left standing in water.

Although the usual way to water a plant is from the top, very dry plants and seedlings are best watered from the bottom. To do this, place the pot in an empty bucket or bowl. Then fill this container with lukewarm water until the water reaches the soil's surface. Then take the pot from the bucket and let it drain.

Watering plants does not add to the humidity around them, but misting does. When the house is dry, spray your moisture-loving plants daily with lukewarm water from a distance of a foot or two. They'll love the shower.

Put your plants around a bucket of water. Run a wick from each plant to the bucket. Water will keep moving from the bucket to the plants while you are gone. (You can buy long wicks at a garden center or hardware store.)

Water your plants thoroughly. Then set them on a pebble tray out of direct sun. Put a long stake along the rim of each plant. Cover the plants with a plastic tent. Tuck the sides of the tent under the tray.

Fertilizing

Just as you need certain vitamins and minerals to stay healthy, plants need certain chemical elements to thrive. They get some of these elements from the water that passes through the soil. Unfortunately, watering washes these chemicals away. So, from time to time, you must fertilize your plant to put important chemicals back into its soil.

Most houseplants need fertilizer once or twice a month during the growing season. However, just as in watering, it's possible for a plant to get too much of a good thing. It's better to fertilize a plant too little than too often. A resting plant should never be fertilized (see page 13).

Fertilizer can be either liquid or powder. Most all-purpose fertilizers will do the job. Follow the instructions on the package for the amount to give your plant. (Use a measuring spoon that is set aside for gardening use only — don't use a kitchen spoon since fertilizer may be poisonous if eaten.)

You can fertilize and water at the same time. Add the measured amount of fertilizer to the water in your watering can. But pour the mixture on damp soil only — never fertilize a plant when it is completely dry. The strong chemicals may "burn" the roots.

Grooming

To groom means to make neat or attractive. You groom yourself by bathing and taking care of your hair, teeth, and nails. Plants need grooming, too.

Removing Old Growth. As leaves and blossoms turn brown and die, pinch or cut them off. Do this as close to the stem as possible. Removing old growth encourages the plant to produce new growth.

Pruning. Occasionally, as stems get too long, you may need to prune your plant. A simple way to do this is to pinch off the leaf buds at the stem ends. Use the fingernails of your thumb and index finger or a scissors. Pruning at the stem ends will stop the growth there and make the plant grow out sideways. The drawing shows where to pinch two kinds of stems.

If a plant gets too out of hand, you may need to ask a grown-up to cut off whole branches or parts of branches. Never do this job yourself. The cuts should be done with a sharp knife right above a node, as shown in the picture. Save the healthy stems you cut from a plant and use them to produce new plants (see page 44).

Turning. Plants grow in the direction of light. To keep your plant growing straight, turn it often.

Cleaning. Plants take in air through pores in their leaves. Dirt and dust on leaves can clog these pores. To keep your plants free of dirt and dust, clean them regularly. Wipe their leaves with a damp cloth or dust them with a soft brush. And, occasionally, give your plants a good shower. Use a rinsing hose, if possible. Set the plant out of the sun to dry. If your plants are really dirty or bothered by insect pests, give them a soapy bath.

How to Bathe a Plant . . . .

Wrap the pot in aluminum foil or a plastic bag. Turn the plant upside down and swish it gently in a bucket of soapy water. Then rinse and set the plant out of the sun to dry.

Letting Your Plants Rest

From time to time, most plants need some kind of rest. Some plants rest by not flowering. Some rest by not growing. Others die back and become completely dormant.

During its resting period, a plant needs very little water or none at all. It also needs no fertilizer.

Most houseplants rest during fall and winter, when days are short — generally from November through February. A few grow actively during this period, however, and rest at other times. It is important to learn the habits of each plant and to recognize when it needs to rest.

An Album of
Twelve Special Plants
by Season

African Violet

LATIN NAME: **Saintpaulia**

BLOOMS YEAR-ROUND

An African violet is a perky plant. It will bloom for you year-round *if*…it has plenty of light… it has plenty of warmth…it has plenty of humidity.

If you get the idea that this plant is fussy about its environment, you are right. It is a native of tropical Africa. Like many tropical plants, it doesn't like drafts, cold, or long spells of cloudy weather. But this should not stop you from trying to grow it. For though the African violet is fussy, it is a good grower. And its fuzzy, velvety leaves are pretty without blooms.

How to Grow an African Violet

NEEDS A PARTLY SUNNY SPOT 🥀 WARM TEMPERATURE 🥀 HIGH HUMIDITY

- Water carefully when the soil begins to dry out but is still damp.
- Provide plenty of humidity. You can mist an African violet if you are careful to use lukewarm water and let it dry in the shade. Otherwise, the leaves may spot.
- Fertilize every two weeks when the plant is growing well. In winter, if growing stops, do not fertilize.
- Groom by removing flowers as they die. Also, dust leaves regularly with a soft brush. Handle the plant with care. Its fleshy stems break easily.
- If you live in a northern area, give the plant more light in winter. Move it to a south-facing window or give it artificial light.

How to Repot. Pot in a shallow, fairly "tight" pot. Use a humusy soil. See pages 42–3.

How to Propagate.
Propagate from leaf cuttings. Also see page 45.

1. Break off a leaf at the stem's base

2. Make a hole at a 45° angle

3. Set the stem ½ inch in soil

African violets are fun to collect and there are many ways to show them off. Line them in a row on a windowsill or shelf. Arrange them on a pebble tray or in a shallow container. Use sturdy glasses, clay pots, or bricks to display your plants at different heights.

Geranium

LATIN NAME: *Pelargonium hortorum*

BLOOMS ALMOST YEAR-ROUND

It has soft, plush leaves and large, bright flower clusters. You find it growing in gardens, in shop windows, on porches, in window boxes, and in houses. It is one of the most popular flowering plants on earth. What is it? It's a geranium.

There are many kinds of geraniums. The most widely grown has leaves shaped like horseshoes.

It is difficult to keep a single geranium blooming year-round. But if you propagate the plant often, you can have blooms most of the year. While one plant rests, another can bloom.

There are as many different ways to grow a geranium as there are to raise a puppy. Everyone seems to have his or her own special rules. You may have to experiment a little to find a way that works for you. But here is a rule that everyone agrees on: give the geranium lots of sun, but don't let it get too hot.

How to Grow a Geranium

NEEDS A SUNNY SPOT MEDIUM DAYTIME TEMPERATURES, COOL NIGHTTIME TEMPERATURES MEDIUM HUMIDITY

- Water only when the soil begins to feel dry.
- Fertilize twice a month during the growing season. If growth slows up in winter, stop fertilizing. Use a fertilizer that is low in nitrogen. Check the label.
- Pinch the plant often to keep it bushy. Geraniums have a habit of getting tall and out of hand if not pinched. Remove only leaf buds, not flower buds.
- Ask a grown-up's help with grooming. Remove the flowers with a sharp knife.

How to Repot. Pot your geranium in a "tight" plastic pot. Use an all-purpose soil. Pack the soil firmly around the roots. See pages 42–3.

How to Propagate. Propagate from seeds or stem cuttings at any time of the year. Cuttings taken in June will bloom in September. See page 44.

Are you a curious scientist? If so, here's an experiment you can try to find out if green plants need sunlight to grow and stay healthy. Tape a piece of dark cloth or paper over one of the leaves of your geranium plant. Care for your plant as usual. After a week, uncover the leaf. What happened to the leaf? What's the explanation?

Hibiscus

LATIN NAME: *Hibiscus*

BLOOMS YEAR-ROUND

In faraway Polynesia the hibiscus is a sacred flower. It is easy to understand why, for this plant produces breathtaking flowers that look like large paper bells.

You might expect such an exotic plant to be hard to grow. But the opposite is true. The hibiscus is one of the easiest flowering plants to grow indoors.

The hibiscus grows in large and small sizes. Dwarf hibiscuses are very popular. They produce flowers in a variety of colors — reds, yellows, oranges, and pinks.

How to Grow a Hibiscus

NEEDS A PARTLY SUNNY SPOT &❧ WARM TEMPERATURES &❧ HIGH HUMIDITY

- Keep moist. Water while soil is still damp but not wet. If the plants are allowed to dry out, they may drop their buds before they open.
- Mist regularly.
- Fertilize once a month.
- Keep the leaves shiny by wiping them often with a damp cloth.
- Pinch back occasionally to keep the plant bushy, and prune if necessary to keep it from getting too tall.

How to Repot. Pot in a plastic pot. Use an all-purpose soil. See pages 42–3.

How to Propagate. Propagate from stem cuttings. Take cuttings from new stems, not old and woody ones. See page 44.

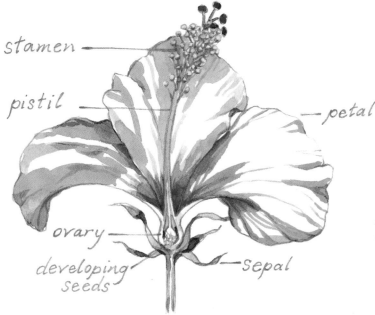

stamen

pistil

petal

ovary

developing seeds

sepal

Make a cross section of a hibiscus blossom and identify the parts. Get a grown-up to help you. With a sharp knife, cut the blossom in half, making sure to divide the roundish pistil. If you're lucky, you may find some developing seeds in the ovary (rounded base) of the pistil.

21

Wax Begonia

LATIN NAME: *Begonia semperflorens*

BLOOMS YEAR-ROUND

You've probably seen them outside in shady garden spots. They have waxy green or red-tipped leaves and small, satiny flowers. They are wax begonias. Their Latin name is *Begonia semperflorens.*

In Latin *semper* means "always" and *florens* means "blooming." Wax begonias may not have large blossoms, but what they don't have in size they make up for in number. These waxy-leaved plants have lots of blossoms all year long.

There are many kinds of wax begonias. Some have single blossoms. Others have double blossoms. The double blossoms look like tiny roses or camellias.

How to Grow a Wax Begonia

NEEDS A PARTLY SUNNY SPOT 🐾 MEDIUM TEMPERATURE 🐾 MEDIUM TO HIGH HUMIDITY

- Water only when the soil begins to dry out. These plants have fleshy stems. They may rot in soggy soil.
- Fertilize twice a month.
- Groom by removing flowers as they die. You can pull or snip them off.
- Pinch the plant often to keep it bushy. If your plant gets too tall, prune it.
- In northern areas, the plant may need a rest in the dead of winter, if light is poor. If so, do not fertilize, and go easy on the water.

How to Repot. Pot your wax begonia in a "tight" shallow pot. Put it in a hanging pot if you like. Use a humusy soil. See pages 42–3.

How to Propagate. Propagate from seeds or stem cuttings. See page 44.

single   double

Can you improve on nature? Plant breeders can through crossbreeding — taking pollen from one plant to fertilize the eggs of another plant. The seeds that develop produce a new kind of plant, one that has some of the characteristics of both parents. For instance, in nature, the wax begonia has only a single set of petals. Crossbreeding has produced begonias with two or more sets of petals. These are called double-blossomed plants.

Amaryllis

LATIN NAME: *Hippeastrum*

BLOOMS IN SPRING FROM WINTER PLANTING

If you want huge, spectacular flowers, an amaryllis is your plant. An amaryllis is a tall, lily-like flower that grows from a bulb. Some amaryllis flowers get to be ten inches across. Most are about five to six inches across.

In winter, you can buy an amaryllis at a flower shop, already potted. Or you can buy the bare bulb and pot it yourself in all-purpose soil. A bulb is an enlarged underground stem that stores food and water. Plants that grow from bulbs die back each year. However, if you store the bulb and replant it the following year, the plant will grow again.

How to Grow an Amaryllis

NEEDS A PARTLY SUNNY SPOT ❧ WARM DAYTIME TEMPERATURES, COOL NIGHTTIME TEMPERATURES ❧ MEDIUM HUMIDITY

- Bottom water the potted bulb thoroughly every two weeks until the flower spike or leaves appear. Then set the pot in a sunny spot and water thoroughly once a week.
- Fertilize once a month during its spring and summer growing season.
- After the buds open in six to eight weeks, move the plant into a partly sunny spot. Continue to water and fertilize as before. The blooms should last many weeks.
- When the flowers fade, ask an adult to cut off each flower at its base with a clean, sharp blade. Move the plant back into a sunny spot. Water and fertilize all summer.
- At summer's end, when the leaves turn yellow, cut them off with clean snippers. Then store the pot on its side in a cool spot in the house until winter. Do not water.

How to Repot. Put the amaryllis bulb in a six-inch pot. Fill the pot about three-fourths full of all-purpose potting soil. Set the bulb on the soil. Add more soil to half cover the bulb. The top part of the bulb should poke out of the soil. Bottom water the potted bulb.
Then place it on a drainage saucer.

How to Propagate. Often, a mature amaryllis bulb will produce "baby" bulbs. Ask an adult to carefully remove these bulbs, using a knife if necessary. Pot them in small pots, the way you would mature bulbs.

The amaryllis is a tender, fair-weather bulb. It is well suited for indoor gardens and can be carried over from one year to the next. Popular garden bulbs such as daffodils, crocuses, and hyacinths are hardy and used to cold winter temperatures, but they are less suited to indoor living. However, nurseries know how to force them to bloom indoors. If someone gives you a pot of hardy bulbs, take care of them as you would an amaryllis. Then in the spring when they have finished blooming, plant them outdoors in your garden. Some may bloom next year.

Orchid Cactus

LATIN NAME: **Epiphyllum ackermanni** or **Phyllocactus ackermanni**

BLOOMS IN SPRING

A cactus is a desert plant with spines, right? Not always! A cactus is a special kind of succulent plant. Most cacti have thick stems that store water. Many have spines, but some do not. Most have no leaves. Most live in deserts, but some live in grassy areas or forests.

The orchid cactus comes from tropical forests. In the forest it perches on trees. It takes its food and water from air and from debris that collects on the tree. Plants that live on other plants this way are called air plants.

Cacti produce some of the most beautiful flowers in the world. The orchid cactus is no exception. It produces huge, dazzling blossoms. These grow from the edges of the plant's long, leaf-like stems.

How to Grow an Orchid Cactus

NEEDS A PARTLY SUNNY SPOT ❧ MEDIUM DAYTIME TEMPERATURES, COOL NIGHTTIME TEMPERATURES ❧ MEDIUM HUMIDITY

- Remember, an orchid cactus is not a desert plant. So keep it on the moist side, not dry. Water when soil begins to dry out but is still damp.
- Fertilize every two weeks during the growing season — April to August. Use a fertilizer low in nitrogen. Check the label.
- Clean by wiping the stems regularly with a damp cloth.
- Let the plant rest from September to March. Water less often and do not fertilize.

How to Repot. Pot in a clay or plastic pot. Because these plants have long, cascading stems, you might choose a hanging pot or one on a stand. Use a humusy soil. See pages 42–3.

How to Propagate. Propagate from stem cuttings in spring or summer. Take the cutting off the end of a stem. Let the cut dry out and scar over. Then place the cutting in a root mixture. See page 44.

In its native tropical habitat, the orchid cactus uses its strong roots to cling to trees, much in the same way ivy clings to a wall.

Shrimp Plant

LATIN NAME: **Beloperone guttata**

BLOOMS IN SUMMER

A plant that produces shrimp? No, these colorful plants can't work miracles. But their hanging orange clusters sure look like shrimp. What these clusters are, really, are special leaves called bracts. The plant's tiny white flowers form at the ends of these bracts.

The shrimp plant, like the hibiscus, has woody stems and can grow quite large. You must pinch it back from time to time to keep it shapely.

How to Grow a Shrimp Plant

NEEDS A SUNNY SPOT ❧ WARM TEMPERATURES ❧ MEDIUM HUMIDITY

- Water a shrimp plant frequently, just as it begins to dry out.
- Fertilize every two weeks in spring and summer, when new leaves are forming.
- Remove bracts as they fade. At the same time, prune the plant to keep it shapely.
- Clean the hairy leaves by brushing.

How to Repot. Pot once a year in a clay or plastic pot. Use an all-purpose soil. See pages 42–3.

How to Propagate. Propagate after the flowering season from stem cuttings about three inches long. See page 44.

It's not a good idea to put a plant in a pot without a drainage hole. Soggy soil is often the result. However, you can use any beautiful container as an outer pot. Just put a layer of small stones or gravel on the bottom of the container for drainage. Then set your potted plant inside.

Strawberry Geranium

LATIN NAME: *Saxifraga sarmentosa*

BLOOMS IN SUMMER

Do you have a cool, east-facing window just waiting for a plant? If so, you might hang a strawberry geranium there. Another name for this plant is strawberry begonia.

The strawberry geranium is neither a geranium nor a begonia, though its hairy leaves make it resemble both these plants. It's not a strawberry, either. However, like a strawberry plant, it sends out long string-like runners. Off the runners, little plantlets grow. When rooted, these plantlets become new plants.

The flowers of a strawberry geranium are not showy. But they are pleasing the way some wildflowers are. Clusters of tiny white flowers grow on top of wiry flower stalks.

How to Grow a Strawberry Geranium

NEEDS A PARTLY SUNNY SPOT &⁊ COOL TEMPERATURES &⁊ MEDIUM TO HIGH HUMIDITY

- Water a strawberry geranium just as it begins to dry out.
- Fertilize only every three to four months.
- When the blooms fade, snip off at the base of the stem.
- Mist often if the room is very dry.

How to Repot. Put in a hanging pot with a drainage saucer. Use an all-purpose soil. See pages 42–3.

How to Propagate. Propagate in spring from runners. See page 45.

You can make your own hanging pot out of a coconut shell. All you need is a coconut, three screw eyes, three pieces of string, and a plastic ring. First, ask an adult to cut the end off the coconut and help you remove the meat. (Use the coconut meat for a tasty snack.) Second, screw in the three screw eyes at equal spaces from each other around the rim of the coconut. Third, thread the ends of the three strings through the holes and tie. Fourth, gather the loose ends of the three strings together and tie them to the plastic ring. Finally, set your potted plant in the coconut shell and hang it on a hook.

Chrysanthemum

LATIN NAME: *Chrysanthemum morifolium* or *hortorum*

BLOOMS IN FALL

"Mum" is the word for this fall bloomer. The short word, that is. These longtime favorites are as much a part of fall as pumpkins and Halloween. In fall, people all across the country grow mums, inside and out.

A chrysanthemum can be hard to keep growing and blooming from one year to the next. But if you propagate your plant from stem cuttings each spring, you can have mums year after year.

How to Grow a Chrysanthemum

NEEDS A SUNNY SPOT ❧ WARM DAYTIME TEMPERATURES, COOL NIGHTTIME TEMPERATURES ❧ HIGH HUMIDITY

- Keep moist. Water while soil is still damp but not wet.
- Mist regularly.
- Pinch the plant back often during the growing season to keep it bushy.
- Fertilize every two weeks during its summer growing season. Stop fertilizing when blooms begin to open in fall.
- Move the plant out of direct sun once it has set buds. The flowers will last longer if you do.
- Groom by removing flowers as they die. You can pull or snip them off.

How to Repot. Pot in a roomy plastic pot. Use an all-purpose soil. See pages 42–3.

How to Propagate. Propagate from seeds or from stem cuttings in spring, or anytime. See page 44.

How can you make your mums last all year? Dry them. All you need is some clean, dry sand, some cornmeal or borax, and a tall box with a lid. For small flowers, an oatmeal or cornmeal box will do. Put an inch or two of sand on the bottom of the box. Anchor the stems of your flowers in the sand so they don't touch one another. Gently sift or spoon more sand in and around the flowers until each is completely covered. Cover the box with the lid and wait a week or two. When the flowers are completely dry, gently remove the sand. Then carefully blow or dust off the flowers with a fine brush and arrange them in a vase.

Spathiphyllum

LATIN NAME: *Spathiphyllum*

BLOOMS IN FALL

A spathiphyllum (SPATH-ee-FIE-lum) is one of the few flowering plants that does well in a sunless room. As long as it is kept warm and moist, it will produce blooms, even in a north-facing window. But don't put it in a dark corner. Even a spathiphyllum needs brightness, if not direct sunlight.

The spathiphyllum does not have a common name, but some gardeners call it a "spathe plant." A spathe is a special petal-like leaf that forms a little bonnet around a flower.

The white, lily-like spathes of a spathiphyllum surround its yellow flower spikes. These blooms last a long time, making a spathiphyllum a very popular plant.

How to Grow a Spathiphyllum

NEEDS A BRIGHT SUNLESS OR PARTLY SUNNY SPOT ❧ MEDIUM TO WARM TEMPERATURES ❧ HIGH HUMIDITY

- Water spathiphyllum often to keep it moist but not soggy.
- Fertilize only every two to three months.
- Mist often, or keep on a pebble tray.
- When its blooms die, ask an adult to cut off the entire flower stalk at its base.
- Keep the leaves shiny by wiping them often with a damp cloth.

How to Repot. Put in a "tight" plastic pot. Use a humusy soil. See pages 42–3.

How to Propagate. Propagate by dividing. See page 45.

If you want to wow your friends, plant three spathiphyllum plants together in one large pot. The result will look like one huge prize-winner!

Kalanchoe

LATIN NAME: ***Kalanchoe blossfeldiana***

BLOOMS IN WINTER

Here's a plant that you can find in bloom at flower shops all year long. But it blooms naturally only in winter. A kalanchoe (kal-an-KO-ee) needs a period of short days in the fall to make it bloom. But the bright, long-lasting blossoms that result make the effort worthwhile.

Even when not blooming, a kalanchoe is a beautiful plant. It has thick, waxy, succulent leaves. If you take care of this plant, it will give you many years of pleasure.

How to Grow a Kalanchoe

NEEDS A SUNNY SPOT ❧ COOL TO MEDIUM TEMPERATURES ❧ MEDIUM HUMIDITY

- Water only when the soil begins to feel dry.
- Fertilize every two weeks when the plant is not in bloom. During its blooming period, fertilize only once a month.
- Clean by wiping the leaves regularly with a damp cloth.
- Pinch back the plant often in spring and summer to keep it bushy.

How to Repot. Pot in a clay pot. Use a sandy soil. See pages 42–3.

How to Propagate. Propagate from seeds or from stem cuttings in early fall. See page 44.

To make a short-day plant bloom, give it fourteen hours of darkness every day for about six weeks during its resting period. (For the kalanchoe, this occurs in September and October.) Do this by covering the plant with a brown paper bag or a black cloth every night about suppertime. Don't remove the cloth until morning. When buds appear, you can stop covering the plant at night. Keep the plant on the dry side during this period and do not fertilize. Instead of using a paper bag, you might set the plant in a closet or dark, unused room.

Christmas Cactus

LATIN NAME: **Schlumbergera bridgesii** or *Zygocactus truncatus*

BLOOMS IN WINTER

For many people, Christmas just isn't Christmas without a Christmas cactus. These beautiful plants produce bright red, pink, or white flowers throughout their flowering season. This begins sometime in December and may last until March.

Like the orchid cactus, the Christmas cactus is a rain-forest plant, not a desert one. In the wild, it grows in trees.

The Christmas cactus has no leaves or spines. Instead, it has many-jointed stems that look like leaves. Flowers grow from the ends of these jointed stems.

How to Grow a Christmas Cactus

NEEDS A BRIGHT SUNLESS OR PARTLY SUNNY SPOT ❧ COOL TEMPERATURES ❧ MEDIUM HUMIDITY

- Remember, a Christmas cactus is not a desert plant. So, like an orchid cactus, keep it on the moist side. Water when the soil is damp.
- Fertilize every two weeks during the growing season — March through August. Use a fertilizer low in nitrogen. Check the label.
- Clean by wiping the stems regularly with a damp cloth.
- Like the kalanchoe, the Christmas cactus is a short-day plant. To set buds it needs a period of short days. Turn to page 37 for directions on how to shorten the days of your plant. Keep the plant on the dry side during its short-day period and do not fertilize. Some gardeners encourage blooming with cool temperatures rather than short days. Keep the plant in a cool room for six weeks before the blooming season. Keep the plant on the dry side during this period and do not fertilize. When buds set, return to its normal spot.

How to Repot. Pot in either a clay or plastic pot. Put in a hanging pot if you wish. Use a humusy soil. See pages 42–3.

How to Propagate. Propagate from stem cuttings. See page 44.

A cactus is a special kind of succulent plant. The most distinguishing feature of a cactus is a tiny organ called an areole. The areole is the growth point of a cactus. All new stems and flowers develop from areoles. The word *areole* is Latin for "little area." To the naked eye, an areole looks like a fuzzy dot. But examine an areole under a magnifying glass and you can see that it looks like a ball of cotton.

Troubleshooting

From time to time, a plant develops troubles. Its leaves may turn pale or yellow. It may fail to bloom. Or, worse, it wilts or rots. Sometimes such troubles are caused by pests or disease. Usually they are caused by poor care.

What should you do if your plant looks troubled? First, think about the care you have been giving the plant. Have you provided the plant with everything it needs? Review the instructions about environment and care at the beginning of this book. If you discover that you are doing something wrong, correct the problem.

Here are some common problems and their likely causes. If

...*leaves and stems wilt*...the plant probably needs water.

...*leaves turn pale or yellow or stems are long or spindly*...the plant may need more light.

...*tips of leaves turn brown*...the plant probably is getting too much or too little water.

...*leaves, flowers, or buds drop off*...the plant probably is getting too much or too little water or fertilizer.

...*the plant never blooms or doesn't produce new leaves or stems*...it probably needs more light.

...*stems rot*...the plant is probably getting too much water.

...*roots grow out of the bottom of the pot*...the plant needs a bigger pot and new soil.

...*leaves have little burn spots*...the plant may be getting too much sun.

...*the plant produces only small leaves*...it may need fertilizer or new soil.

...*green scum or white crust forms in or on the pot*...the plant is getting too much fertilizer.

...*leaves turn black or are covered with mildew or ugly spots*...the plant may have a disease.

When Disease Is the Trouble

If you think your plant's trouble is disease, cut off all damaged leaves and stems. Move the plant away from other plants and give it proper care. If the plant continues to look sickly, throw it out, soil and all. Then buy a new plant.

When Pests Are the Trouble

If your plants are healthy and well cared for, chances are good that pests won't attack them. But sometimes pests get into the home aboard other plants. If you notice little crawling or scaly insects on your plant or white, cottony material, give the plant a soapy bath (see page 13). Then keep it isolated and check the plant regularly throughout the next month. If the pests reappear, dab them with a cotton swab that has been dipped in rubbing alcohol. Repeat this treatment every few days until the pests are gone.

If none of these treatments works, throw the plant away.

Some Common Plant Pests

INSECT		DESCRIPTION	WHAT TO DO
Aphids		Tiny lice-like insects with long legs. Some have wings.	Dab pests with a cotton swab soaked in rubbing alcohol. Or spray with a mixture of one part alcohol and one part water. Or spray off with a rinsing hose. Or wash off in a soapy bath. Repeat treatment every few days until pests are gone.
Mealy Bugs		Tiny oval-shaped insects with a white powdery coat. Make nests of white cottony material.	Treat as above.
Red Spider Mites		Tiny hard-to-see red spider-like insects. Make webs that stretch from leaf to leaf or stem to stem.	Spray off with a rinsing hose. Or wash off in a soapy bath. Repeat treatment as necessary.
Scale		Tiny flat insects with shell-like coats.	Wash off or scrub off with a toothbrush dipped in soapy water. Repeat treatment as necessary.
White Flies		Tiny white flying insects. Young ones look something like scale.	Treat young white flies as you would scale. Spray off mature insects with a rinsing hose. Or try to clap them between your hands. Repeat treatment as necessary.

Potting Your Plants

When you buy a plant, it comes already potted in soil that is right for it. However, from time to time, a plant outgrows its pot or needs new soil. Then you will need to repot it. A sure sign your plant needs repotting is roots coming out the drainage hole. Gardeners say such a plant is pot-bound, or root-bound.

You don't need a fancy pot for your plant. A simple clay or plastic pot with a drainage hole and drainage saucer will do. Just make sure the pot is a little bigger than the root ball of your plant. One that is too big will hold water too long; one that is too small won't hold water long enough. A few plants like a "tight" pot — that is, they like their roots to be held tightly.

What kind of soil should you use? Most garden soils are not right for potted plants. They are too heavy and don't have the right combination of grit and humus. So you must buy potting soil for your plants. Most of the plants in this book need either humusy soil or all-purpose soil. Some succulents need sandy soil.

Repotting is messy business. What's the best way to do it? Before you begin, spread your work area with newspapers and put on some old work clothes. Next gather everything you need and prepare the new pot for planting.

First make sure the pot is clean. Dirty pots may harbor disease or insect pests. Next place a broken piece of crockery over the drainage hole. This will keep the hole from clogging. Cover the crock with a layer of soil.

Now water the plant and carefully remove it from its old pot. To do this, place the fingers of one hand around the stem of the plant and over the top of the pot. Hold the base of the pot with the other hand. Then loosen the root ball by turning the pot upside down and knocking it gently against a hard surface. Finally, pull the pot upward away from the plant and let the plant drop into your hand.

Place the root ball of your plant in the pot you have prepared and hold it in place. Then spoon more soil around the plant. Press the soil around the root ball gently to secure the plant in place. Add more soil if needed so that the soil is at the proper level. This should be about an inch from the rim of the pot.

Water the plant well. If necessary, rinse off its leaves. Then set the plant on a drainage saucer and place it out of the sun to drain.

Multiplying Your Plants

What's better than one beautiful plant? Two beautiful plants. Propagating your plants, or making them multiply, can be loads of fun. Some people think it's the best part of gardening.

Most houseplants can be propagated from seeds or from cuttings. You will need a special rooting mixture. Most potting soils are not right for propagating. You can use moistened peat moss or sand. Or mix equal parts of moistened peat moss and sand (or perlite) or mix equal parts of potting soil and vermiculite (or perlite).

You can buy houseplant seeds at garden centers or order them from a gardening catalog. Be sure to read the planting instructions on the package.

Before you plant your seeds, partly fill a shallow pot with the rooting mixture. Then arrange the seeds in the pot. Cover large seeds with a thin layer of mixture but leave tiny seeds uncovered. Water the pot from the bottom and let it drain. Before setting the pot in a warm, sunless spot, cover it with a clear plastic bag. Water the pot from time to time to keep it moist. When the seedlings have two pairs of leaves, remove the plastic bag. Pull out all but a few of the strongest seedlings and set the pot in a suitable spot. Continue to water it. When the seedlings are big enough to handle, transfer each to its own pot.

Propagating plants from cuttings is the fastest way to get mature plants. There are four ways to do this: from stem cuttings, from leaf cuttings, from runners, and by dividing.

From stem cuttings. Ask a grown-up to take a cutting from the end of a healthy new stem, cutting below the node. Remove the lower leaves and take off any flowers or flower buds. Leave the leaf buds. Fill a small pot with rooting mixture and moisten the mixture. Plant the cutting in the mixture or propagate it in water until roots form. Then pot it in suitable soil. Water the cutting and set it aside to drain. When the cutting has drained, cover it, pot and all, with a clear plastic bag. Set the plant in a bright, sunless spot and water it from time to time to keep it moist. After several weeks, test to see if the cutting has roots. (Gently tug on it. If the cutting resists, it has roots.) When it's rooted, pot the cutting in suitable potting soil. Water it. Then move the plant to a warm spot and give it normal care.

From leaf cuttings. Ask a grown-up to cut off a healthy leaf, leaving about two inches of stem. Put the leaf into a jar of water. (Or propagate the leaf in soil, as you would a stem cutting.) Hold it in place with a clip or aluminum foil. Set the pot in a bright, sunless spot. Add water as necessary. In four to eight weeks, the leaf will develop little plantlets. When these are big enough to handle, pot each in suitable soil. Water them. Move the plants to a suitable spot and give them normal care.

From runners. Place a small pot filled with rooting mixture near the parent plant. Find a plantlet at the end of a runner. Set it on the mixture. Hold it in place with a hairpin or clip. Water the plantlet regularly to keep it moist. When new leaves appear on the plantlet, cut it from the parent plant. Continue to water it regularly. When the plant is large enough to handle, pot it in suitable soil. Water it. Give it normal care.

By dividing. Remove the plant from its pot. Shake away loose soil and gently pull its crowns apart. Or cut away the plantlet. Repot the old plant and pot the new one in suitable soil. Water the plants well. Set them in a bright, sunless spot. When growth begins, move them to a suitable spot. Give them normal care.

Glossary

Artificial light Light produced by electricity, not the sun. Fluorescent and special plant-growing bulbs produce light that promotes plant growth.

Bud An undeveloped flower or leaf. A flower bud looks different from a leaf bud. It is wrapped tightly in a calyx of sepals. As the bud opens, the sepals are pushed apart to expose the petals inside. On some plants, flower buds appear only at the tips of stems. On other plants, buds also form along the sides of stems.

Calyx A collection of sepals

Corolla A collection of petals

Crockery Clay pots and other earthenware

Crown Main stem; part of plant where stem and roots join

Cutting A part of a plant that has been cut off and prepared for rooting

Direct sun Unfiltered sunlight that falls directly on a plant; strong sunlight

Dormant Resting, not growing

Fertilize To give a plant fertilizer; to cause to produce seeds

Fertilizer Plant food

Flower A seed-producing organ, typically composed of four parts — petals, sepals, stamens, and a pistil

Humidity Air moisture

Humus The spongy material in soil made from decayed plant and animal remains

Long-day plants Plants that need a period of long days to produce buds

Lukewarm Barely warm, tepid; feels neither warm nor cold

Mist Spray with a fine shower of water

Node The place along a stem where a leaf or flower bud forms

Parent plant A mature (adult) plant

Petals The showy part of a flower. They are often brightly colored. All the petals together form the corolla.

Photosynthesis Process by which plants make their own food using energy from sunlight, gases from the air, and water from the soil.

Pistil The female part of the flower. It is in the base of the pistil that seeds develop.

Pot-bound A plant's roots have outgrown the pot

Propagate To make multiply. Most plants can be propagated from seeds or from cuttings.

Prune To cut or pinch off plant parts for the purpose of improving its looks

Root ball A plant's ball-shaped network of roots

Seedling The young plant that develops from a seed

Short-day plants Plants that need a period of short days to produce buds — generally less than twelve hours of daylight a day. You can shorten a plant's day by putting it in a dark closet at suppertime or covering it with a black cloth or with a brown paper bag. Don't forget to repeat this action every night without fail. Even a few seconds of light at the wrong time can ruin the cycle of short days.

Stamen The male part of the flower. It produces the yellow substance called pollen. A single flower may have many pollen-making stamens.

Succulent A type of plant with special water-holding abilities. Many can hold water in stems and leaves for long periods of time, making them able to live through long dry spells.

Tight pot A pot that barely fits the root ball of a plant. Some plants do better squeezed into a pot that can hold only a small amount of soil and water than in a larger pot that holds more soil and water.